The Cookie Thief

by Jenny Jinks and Andy Catling

W
FRANKLIN WATTS
LONDON•SYDNEY

Chapter 1

Amari looked at the freshly baked cookies that he and Gran had made.

Dad came into the kitchen. "Ooh, cookies," he said. "They smell delicious!"
He picked one up but dropped it again straight away. It was so hot that it burnt his fingers.

"You can't have any yet," Amari said.

"They are too hot."

Amari put the cookies on the windowsill.

He had to wait for them to cool down

before he could eat them.

5

After a while, Amari thought, "They must be cool by now."

But when he and Gran went to check, Amari got a surprise. The tray on the windowsill was empty. The cookies had gone!

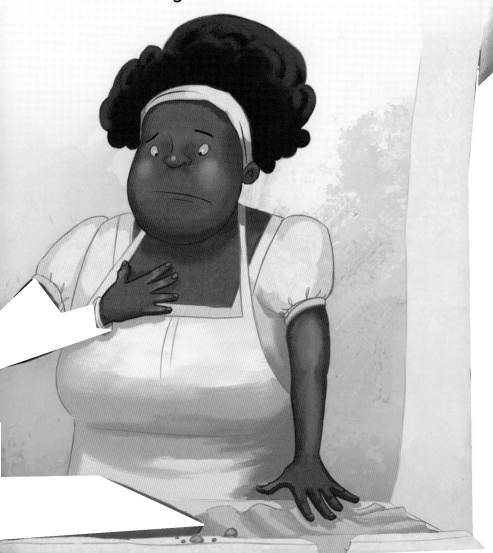

Chapter 2

"Somebody's stolen the cookies!" Amari cried.

"Who would do that?" said Gran.

"I don't know," said Amari. "But I'm going

to find out."

Then Amari remembered ... Dad!

Dad was sitting on the sofa reading the paper ...

and he was licking his fingers.

"Aha!" Amari cried. "Caught you!"

Dad jumped. "What's going on?" he asked.

"You stole the cookies," Amari said.

"No, I didn't," Dad said.

"But you tried to take one earlier," said Amari.

"And you have crumbs down your shirt."

"I was just eating my lunch," laughed Dad,

brushing the crumbs away. "Look!"

He pointed to his plate, with half a sandwich on it.

Amari looked surprised. He had been so sure

it was Dad.

Chapter 3

Amari went back to the kitchen.

He looked at the empty cookie tray,

searching for clues. There were a lot of crumbs.

But only on one side – the side next to

the open window.

He looked into the garden, straight at ...

... Mum!

Mum was digging in the garden.

Amari marched straight up to her.

"Aha!" Amari said. "It was you!"

"What was me?" asked Mum.

"You stole the cookies!" Amari said.

"I haven't seen any cookies," Mum said.

"I've been out here digging."

Amari scratched his head. Who else could it be?

Gran? But she had helped make them.

It didn't make sense.

Amari went back inside. He sat at the table to

think. Then he had an idea.

"Now I know how to catch the cookie thief,"

he said. "Will you help me, Gran?"

Gran nodded, and they got to work.

Chapter 4

Gran pulled the tray of fresh cookies

out of the oven.

"Mmmm," said Amari. These smelled even better

than the first lot.

Gran put them on the windowsill to cool, just like

last time. Then Amari hid under the kitchen table.

He was going to catch the cookie thief in the act.

Amari waited and waited.

Mum came into the kitchen.

Amari watched her carefully.

She made herself a cup of tea and then left.

She did not touch the cookies.

Then Dad came in. Amari watched him.

But Dad just started making dinner.

He did not touch the cookies.

Amari watched Dad chopping and stirring.

He was starting to feel hungry.

Maybe he could have just one cookie?

Amari crept out from under the table.

But when he got to the tray,

the cookies were all gone! Again!

How did this keep happening?

Chapter 5

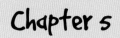

This time, the thief had left a trail of crumbs.

They led across the garden.

Amari followed the trail to a big tree.

He peered up into the tree

and couldn't believe what he saw.

A monkey was up in the branches.

She was feeding Amari's cookies to her babies.

Amari didn't feel cross any more. He didn't mind
that the monkey had taken his cookies.

He watched the monkeys for ages until
Dad called him in for dinner.

When they had finished dinner, Amari said,

"I'm sorry I thought you all stole my cookies,

but I've found out who it was. Come on, I've got

a surprise for you."

He led everyone out into the garden.

"Look," Amari said. They all watched and laughed

as the monkeys played in the tree.

"And I've got a surprise for you," said Gran.

She was carrying a tray of cookies.

"Now we can all have cookies."

"Delicious! Thanks, Gran," said Amari.

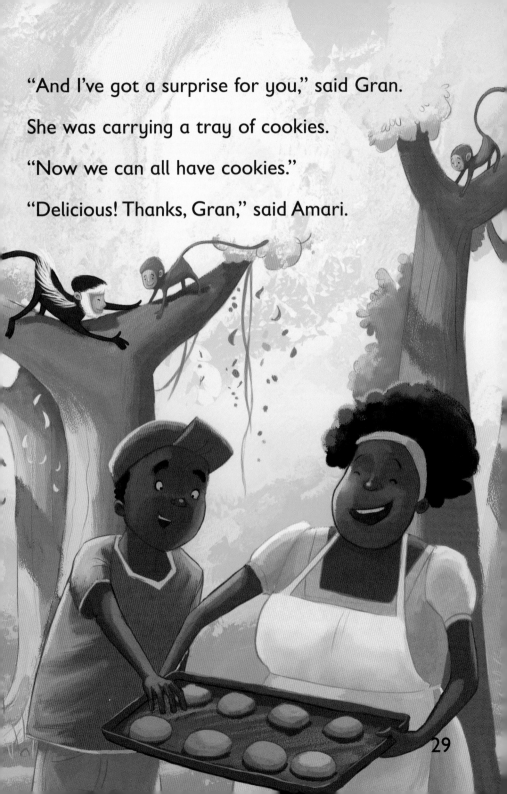

Things to think about

1. Why does Amari think his dad stole the cookies?
2. Why does Amari think his mum stole the cookies?
3. Who did you think the cookie thief might be?
4. Have you ever thought someone has done something wrong when they haven't? Or has someone blamed you for something that wasn't your fault?
5. Which animal would you most like to have living near your home?

Write it yourself

One of the themes of this story is that you should not blame someone for something they have not done.
Can you write a story with a similar theme?

Plan your story before you begin to write it.
Start off with a story map:

- a beginning to introduce the characters and where your story is set (the setting);
- a problem which the main characters will need to fix;
- an ending where the problems are resolved.

Get writing! Try to use interesting ways to show how your characters are feeling, such as *scratched his head*.

Notes for parents and carers

Independent reading

This series is designed to provide an opportunity for your child to read independently, for pleasure and enjoyment. These notes are written for you to help your child make the most of this book.

About the book

Amari has been baking cookies with his grandmother, but every time he leaves them to cool, they disappear. Who is the mysterious cookie thief? Amari is determined to find out and makes a surprising discovery.

Before reading

Ask your child why they have selected this book. Look at the title and blurb together. What do they think it will be about? Do they think they will like it?

During reading

Encourage your child to read independently. If they get stuck on a word, remind them that they can sound it out in syllable chunks. They can also read on in the sentence and think about what would make sense.

After reading

Support comprehension and help your child think about the messages in the book that go beyond the story, using the questions on the page opposite. Give your child a chance to respond to the story, asking:

- Did you enjoy the story and why?
- Who was your favourite character?
- What was your favourite part?
- What did you expect to happen at the end?

Franklin Watts
First published in Great Britain in 2020
by The Watts Publishing Group

Series Editors: Jackie Hamley and Melanie Palmer
Series Advisors: Dr Sue Bodman and Glen Franklin
Series Designers: Cathryn Gilbert and Peter Scoulding

A CIP catalogue record for this book is
available from the British Library.

ISBN 978 1 4451 7237 8 (hbk)
ISBN 978 1 4451 7242 2 (pbk)
ISBN 978 1 4451 7248 4 (library ebook)
ISBN 978 1 4451 7906 3 (ebook)

Printed in China

Franklin Watts
An imprint of
Hachette Children's Group
Part of The Watts Publishing Group
Carmelite House
50 Victoria Embankment
London EC4Y 0DZ

An Hachette UK Company
www.hachette.co.uk

www.reading-champion.co.uk